EASTERN   MOUN

RAT CREATURE
TEMPLE

CONKLE'S
HOLLOW

UPPER PAWA

PAWA

PRAYER
STONE HILL

TANEN GARD

FLINT
RIDGE

THE
GREAT BASIN

PAWA ROAD

ATHEIA

G U L C H

SINNER'S
ROCK

Dreaming of Harvestar

"Jeff Smith can pace a joke better than almost anyone in comics." —Neil Gaiman, author of **Coraline**

"I love **BONE**! **BONE** is great!" —Matt Groening, creator of **The Simpsons**

"**BONE** moves from brash humor to gripping adventure in a single panel." —ALA Booklist

"**BONE** is a comic-book sensation. . . . [It] is a classic of writer-artist craftsmanship not to be missed." —Comics Buyer's Guide

OTHER **BONE** BOOKS

Out from Boneville

The Great Cow Race

Eyes of the Storm

The Dragonslayer

Rock Jaw: Master of the Eastern Border

Old Man's Cave

Ghost Circles

TREASURE HUNTERS

BY JEFF SMITH

WITH COLOR BY STEVE HAMAKER

An Imprint of

■SCHOLASTIC

This book is for Kathleen Glosan

The chapters in this book were originally published in the comic book *BONE* and are copyright © 2001 and 2002 by Jeff Smith. *BONE*® is © 2008 by Jeff Smith.

Library of Congress Catalog Card Number 9568403.
ISBN-13 978-0-439-70630-8 — ISBN-10 0-439-70630-0
ISBN 0-439-70633-5 (paperback)

ACKNOWLEDGMENTS

Harvestar Family Crest designed by Charles Vess
Map of *The Valley* by Mark Crilley
Color by Steve Hamaker

10 9 8   13 14

First Scholastic edition, August 2008
Book design by David Saylor
Printed in Singapore 46

CONTENTS

WHY WAIT? WE HAVE MORE THAN ENOUGH WATER TO REACH **ATHEIA.**

WE HAVE ENOUGH PROVISIONS FOR A **ONE-WAY** JOURNEY.

WHAT DO YOU PROPOSE WE DO . . .

. . . IF ATHEIA **DIDN'T** SURVIVE THE EXPLOSION?

HMM?

LUCIUS THINKS IT DID. AND AS LONG AS I'VE KNOWN HIM, HE'S ALWAYS BEEN RIGHT.

THE SOLDIERS DON'T TRUST HIM.

BUT THE VILLAGERS **DO.** I'LL REMIND YOU THAT LUCIUS DOWN IS A PERSONAL FRIEND OF MINE.

WE KNOW THERE WAS TROUBLE BACK WHEN HE WAS CAPTAIN OF THE GUARD. SOMETHING ABOUT A **ROMP** WITH THE ROYAL SISTERS. BUT OUT HERE, WE DON'T **CARE.**

I'M NOT TALKING ABOUT A ROYAL **SCANDAL.**

I WAS **WITH** CAPTAIN DOWN THAT NIGHT FIFTY YEARS AGO, AND I SAW WHAT HE DID.

HE MARCHED OUR ARMY STRAIGHT INTO A **RAT CREATURE TRAP.** THE BLOODBATH THAT FOLLOWED WAS THE BEGINNING OF THE **GREAT WAR** ITSELF.

YOU WERE AMBUSHED. SO WHAT?

THE RAT CREATURES COULD NOT HAVE AMBUSHED US WITHOUT INSIDE KNOWLEDGE OF OUR ROUTE.

WHY WOULD HE DO IT? LUCIUS DOESN'T LIKE RAT CREATURES. HE **FIGHTS** THEM!

HE WAS THE ONLY ONE WHO KNEW OUR ROUTE THAT NIGHT.

ONLY HE COULD HAVE ALERTED THE ENEMY.

FIFTY YEARS LATER, WHERE'S YOUR **PROOF?!**

A YOUNG FARMER NAMED **JONATHAN OAKS** HAS GIVEN US OUR PROOF.

JON - - ?

OH, BLOODY STARS.

JUST EIGHT DAYS AGO, YOUNG JONATHAN WITNESSED LUCIUS IN THE ARMS OF OUR ENEMY, THE **HOODED ONE** - -

- - DOING **NOTHING** WHILE OUR TROOPS WERE ATTACKED BY RAT CREATURES.

I BELIEVE JONATHAN TOLD YOU THE SAME STORY HE TOLD US.

YES. AND LUCIUS HIMSELF TOLD ME THAT THE HOODED ONE IS ACTUALLY PRINCESS BRIAR - - ONE OF THE TWO **ROYAL SISTERS.**

YES . . .

WHICH BRINGS US TO THE DISCOVERY OF THE **TRACKS** . . .

TREASURE HUNTERS

RIGHT! BACK TO TH' PLAN! WE STILL HAVE TO FIND HATS AND CLOTHES TO TAKE BACK TO PHONEY AND SMILEY.

SPEAKING OF WHICH . . . WHERE DID YOU GET **THAT** HAT?

YOU LIKE IT? I GOT IT FROM THAT GUY.

YOU KNOW, FONE BONE, THE MORE I LOOK AROUND, THE LESS WORRIED I AM THAT WE'LL **STICK OUT** HERE.

YOU THINK?

IT COULD BE WORSE. THERE COULD BE **RAT CREATURES** HERE!

C'MON, THORN. LET'S FIND YOUR GRAN'MA.

FONE BONE, LOOK AT THAT.

THE CARVING ON THAT SHRINE . . .

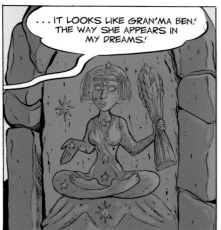

. . . IT LOOKS LIKE GRAN'MA BEN! THE WAY SHE APPEARS IN MY DREAMS!

REALLY?

WELL, WITHOUT THE STARS -- BUT **YOUNG**, AND WITH THAT SAME CROWN.

LET'S TAKE A CLOSER PEEK.

REMARKABLE. THIS LOOKS JUST LIKE MY DREAM.

IT IS NOT SO REMARKABLE.

THIS IS **VEN**, THE **QUEEN** OF DREAMS.

VEN! THE FIRST HUMAN QUEEN.

WOULD YOU LIKE TO MAKE AN OFFERING?

MY PRAYER STONES ARE OF THE HIGHEST QUALITY.

AN OFFERING?

A SMALL OFFERING. ONLY AS MUCH AS YOU FEEL MOVED TO MAKE.

I HAVE MANY BEAUTIFUL STONES. HERE! SEE FOR YOURSELF!

VERY HIGH QUALITY.

THEY **ARE** BEAUTIFUL.

TELL ME, SISTER, ARE YOU A NORTHERNER?

YES.

I CAN TELL BY YOUR ACCENT.

EXCUSE ME. WHO'S ON THIS SHRINE?

THIS IS **MIM**, THE FIRST DRAGON. YOU SEE HER LONG BODY? SHE HOLDS HER TAIL IN HER MOUTH AND GIVES LIFE TO THE WORLD.

AND WHO IS THIS?

THIS IS ALSO MIM -- BUT IN HER DARK ASPECT.

HERE SHE IS THE LORD OF **DEATH**: THE LORD OF THE LOCUSTS.

INTERESTING.

SHE IS THE CREATOR **AND** THE DESTROYER. . .

YOU CANNOT HAVE LIFE WITHOUT DEATH. THE TWO ARE ALWAYS TOGETHER.

THE PRAYER ON THE STONE SEEKS A BALANCE BETWEEN THEM.

THERE IS AN AIR OF BALANCE ABOUT **YOU**, NORTHERN SISTER.

TELL ME, WHY HAVE I NOT SEEN YOUR FACE HERE BEFORE TODAY?

WHAT DO YOU MEAN?

WHAT **MIRACLE** HAS ALLOWED YOU TO PASS THROUGH THE GHOST CIRCLES THAT SURROUND OUR CITY? HOW HAVE YOU REACHED US IN OUR PART OF THE VALLEY?

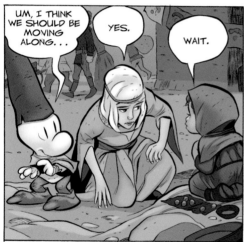

UM, I THINK WE SHOULD BE MOVING ALONG...

YES.

WAIT.

GIVE ME YOUR HAND.

KEEP THIS.

SPOOKY KID. WHAT'D SHE GIVE YOU?

A PRAYER STONE - - 🔆

oh, NO.

OH, NO, WHAT?

OH, NO, **THAT!**

oh, No! **PHONEY BONE AND SMILEY!** THEY WERE SUPPOSED TO WAIT FOR US ON THE OUTSKIRTS OF TOWN.'

WHERE DID THEY GET THAT OX CART?

I'M **TELLIN'** YOU, YOU CAN'T **HAVE** ANY HAY!

BUT I WANT TO BUY IT! WHY DID YOU BRING YOUR HAY TO **MARKET** IF YOU DON'T WANT TO **SELL** IT?

WE LIKE THE **SMELL** OF IT, RIGHT, PHONEY?

YEAH, THAT'S RIGHT. WE LOVE THE MUSTY SMELL OF MILDEWED STRAW. WE LIKE TO KEEP IT NEAR US . . . NOW **SHOVE OFF!**

THERE'S NOTHIN' IN TH' HAY.

PHONCIBLE?

DON'T LOOK AT ME. I GOT NOTHIN' TO DO WITH THIS.

SMILEY...

WHAT?

DO YOU HAVE THAT BABY RAT CREATURE HIDDEN UNDER THERE?

WE COULDN'T LEAVE HIM ALL ALONE, GRAN'MA. HE'S ONLY ONE AN' A HALF YEARS OLD!

SMILEY BONE, YOU TURN THIS CART AROUND **RIGHT NOW** AND GET THAT THING OUT OF TOWN BEFORE YOU GET US ALL KILLED!

I CAN'T **DO** THAT, GRAN'MA. BARTLEBY DEPENDS ON ME! I HAVE TO TAKE CARE OF HIM!

THIS ISN'T A **REQUEST** -- GET THAT CREATURE OUT OF HERE!

NO!

NO?!!

SMILEY--

I'M SORRY, FONE BONE, BUT IT WOULDN'T BE RIGHT. BARTLEBY SAVED OUR **LIVES!** IT JUST WOULDN'T BE RIGHT.

WHY, **YOU** --

PARDON ME, MA'AM.

YES?

I HEAR YOU WANT TO BUY A **COYOTE?**

WHO SENT YOU?

WILLIAM THE BAKER.

THE GHOST CIRCLES AND THE CROWDS ARE MAKING THE CITY LEADERS NERVOUS. VERY FEW OUTSIDERS ARE ALLOWED THROUGH THE GATES.

CAN YOU GET US INSIDE THE CITY-- PAST THE GUARDS, WITHOUT ANY QUESTIONS?

HOW MANY IN YOUR PARTY?

FIVE.

FIVE PLUS A **HAY CART.**

A HAY CART WILL NOT BE SO EASY.

DO YOU KNOW ANYONE ON THE INSIDE? PERHAPS THAT WILL HELP. . .

I DO, BUT I HAVE HAD NO CONTACT WITH ANYONE INSIDE THE CITY FOR NEARLY A YEAR.

MUCH HAS CHANGED IN THE LAST YEAR - - - - ⚡

EXCUSE ME, MISS. MAY I SEE THAT?

MM?

OH. YES.

WHERE DID YOU GET THIS STONE?

FROM THE LITTLE GIRL OVER BY THE SHRINES.

THAT IS TANEAL. SHE IS MY SISTER.

AND SHE IS A **VERY** GOOD JUDGE OF CHARACTER.

COME WITH ME.

OKAY, BOYS, JUMP UP ON TOP.

HMM. I DON'T SEEM TO SEE ANY GOLD PAVEMENT.

sniff! sniff! PEE-YEW! I THINK TH' STREETS ARE PAVED WITH SEWAGE!

SETTLE DOWN . . .

THE TINGLE IN MY SCALP CAN ONLY MEAN **ONE THING!**

THERE'S **TREASURE** HERE OR MY NAME'S NOT **PHONCIBLE P. BONE!**

DEAR, MAY I SEE THE STONE THAT TANEAL GAVE TO YOU?

MM. IT'S COVERED IN SECRET WRITING.

A SECRET PRAYER STONE? STRANGE. WHAT DOES THAT MEAN?

I DON'T KNOW, BUT I HAVE AN OLD FRIEND WHO RUNS A SMALL ROOFTOP KITCHEN WHO MIGHT BE ABLE TO TELL US.

WATCH YOUR STEP.

FONE BONE, DO YOU THINK BARTLEBY IS OKAY IN THE STABLE? NO ONE WILL FIND HIM, WILL THEY?

HE HAS WATER AND FOOD, AND WE LOCKED THE DOOR. AS LONG AS HE DOESN'T MAKE ANY NOISE, HE'LL BE FINE.

OOG! IT SMELLS WORSE UP HERE THAN IT DID ON THE **STREET!**

COME.

EAT.

YOU LAUGH AT **FATE**, YOU MISERABLE LITTLE CREATURE?

NOBODY ROLLS THE DICE FOR **ME**, PAL. THE ONLY DANGER WITHIN US IS THIS **SLOP** YOU'RE DISHIN' OUT!

OUTRAGEOUS!

PHONCIBLE, THIS MAN IS MY TEACHER! HE IS RESPECTED BY THE WISE AS A GREAT **DREAMING MASTER!**

APPARENTLY THE **WISE** DON'T KNOW ABOUT **REFRIGERATION**. YOU TRYIN' TO GIVE US **FOOD POISONING**, OLD MAN?

THIS **SLOP**, YOU **IMP**, IS A TRADITIONAL **PAWANIAN DISH** -- IT TAKES FOURTEEN **DAYS** JUST TO **CURDLE!**

MASTER, PLEASE --

WE HAVE SEEN A GREAT DISASTER IN THE NORTH. **ASH** FALLS FROM THE SKY, AND THE VALLEY IS FILLING WITH GHOSTLY POCKETS OF **CRUELTY** AND **SORROW**. . .

. . . I HAVE COME TO SEEK YOUR COUNSEL AND TO LEARN THE STATE OF AFFAIRS WITHIN THE WALLS OF OUR GREAT CITY.

THE PEOPLE ARE FRIGHTENED.

THE GHOST CIRCLES THAT SURROUND US FORETELL THE COMING OF THE **LOCUST.**

ISN'T THERE ANYTHING IN OUR **LORE** THAT MIGHT TELL US HOW TO ESCAPE OUR DOOM?

YOU WERE NEVER THE MOST ATTENTIVE PUPIL, YOUR MAJESTY. YOU PREFERRED THE **STABLES** TO YOUR LESSONS. YOU HAD A PARTICULAR FONDNESS FOR **COWS**, AS I RECALL.

I'LL TAKE THAT AS A NO. YOUR KITCHEN LOOKS NEGLECTED, OLD FRIEND. HAS SOMETHING **HAPPENED?**

WHEN MY NATIVE **PAWA** DECLARED ITSELF FOR THE LOCUST, MY CUISINE AND I FELL OUT OF **FAVOR.**

MUCH HAS CHANGED...

I SHOULD NEVER HAVE LEFT.

THE INNER COUNCIL THAT WATCHED OVER THE CITY HAS BEEN DISSOLVED. THEY HAVE BEEN REPLACED BY DISCIPLES OF VENU WHO CALL THEMSELVES THE **VEDU.**

VEDU?

THE **EYE?**

THE ORDER OF THE DREAMING EYE. THEY ACCEPT AS TRUTH ONLY THE TEACHINGS OF **VEN**, THE HUMAN QUEEN.

THEY HAVE OUTLAWED ALL DRAGON LORE.

WHAT? HOW CAN THEY SEPARATE **VEN** FROM THE **DRAGONS?** VEN WAS **TAUGHT** BY THE DRAGONS!

BE **CAREFUL**, YOUR HIGHNESS. SUCH WORDS WILL GET YOU ARRESTED OR **WORSE!** THE VEDU BELIEVE THE DRAGONS ARE **ANIMALS**, AND ARE **IMPURE.**

HOW DID THIS HAPPEN?

I'M VERY SORRY, YOUR MAJESTY.

NO, MASTER, IT IS YOU WHO MUST FORGIVE **US**. I SWEAR TO YOU THAT I WILL NOT LEAVE YOU ALONE AGAIN.

THORN, PLEASE BRING OUT THE PRAYER STONE YOU RECEIVED AT THE SHRINE.

FONE BONE HAS IT.

GOT IT!

HERE IT IS ⚡

THAT'S STRANGE! I WALKED THROUGH A **COLD** SPOT.

YES. . . THIS IS ONE OF OURS. IT IS A SECRET TALISMAN FOR THOSE OF US WHO **RESIST** THE VEDU.

HOW INTERESTING THAT IT SHOULD COME INTO YOUR GRANDDAUGHTER'S POSSESSION.

IT SAYS:

MOONWORT.

MOON.

A MOST **BELOVED** RULER.

WHO?

THORN'S MOTHER.

IN TIMES OF DARKNESS, HER THOUGHTS WERE ALWAYS FOR HER **PEOPLE** FIRST--

FONE BONE! LOOK OUT!

WHAT?

IT'S BRIAR! SHE'S HERE!

ARE YOU **SURE? WHERE?**

WE DON'T SEE HER!

STOP...

YOUR WILL IS NO LONGER YOUR OWN, PRINCESS . . . .

THE LOCUST SUMMONS YOU.

GET UP.

A **SHADOW!** RIGHT WHERE THE COLD SPOT IS! DO YOU SEE IT?

LOOK AT THORN!

SHE'S WALKING TOWARD US -- IN A **TRANCE!**

oh, BOY~

THORN! ARE YOU ALL RIGHT?

I -- ☀

YES. SHE'S GONE.

HAS THIS HAPPENED BEFORE?

NO. WHAT **WAS** THAT?

I'VE NEVER WITNESSED ANYTHING LIKE IT. THE LOCUST JUST ATTEMPTED TO STEAL YOUR GRANDDAUGHTER -- RIGHT IN FRONT OF US.'

IN THE HEART OF THE **SACRED CITY!**

THIS IS A NEW KIND OF WARFARE.

ISN'T THIS WHAT WE WERE WORRIED ABOUT?

I'M TAKING HER BACK TO THE ROOM.

DO NOT LEAVE HER ALONE FOR EVEN AN INSTANT.

I WON'T. AND IT MIGHT BE BEST IF YOU CALLED TOGETHER ANY MEMBERS OF THE INNER COUNCIL WHO ARE STILL LOYAL.

IT WILL BE DONE.

JUST A MOMENT, YOUNG FELLOW. TELL ME **EXACTLY** WHAT YOU SAW.

WHO, ME?

I SAW A BLURRY SHADOW ON THE ROOF.

YOU SAW A **BLURRY SHADOW.**

YEAH, DIDN'T YOU?

HMMF.

I WAS TOO BUSY SAVING THE PRINCESS TO REALLY **LOOK**, NOW WASN'T I?

I'LL SEND A MESSENGER AS SOON AS THE INNER COUNCIL IS ASSEMBLED.

I THINK IT WOULD BE BEST IF YOU TRY TO KEEP HER AWAKE.

YES, THANK YOU. GOOD NIGHT, TEACHER.

I REGRET I HAVE NO LUXURIES TO OFFER YOU . . . . NO CUSHIONS TO SIT UPON . . . . . . NO WINE TO DRINK . . .

. . . IT IS MY BELIEF . . . THAT MATERIAL NEEDS ARE A SIGN OF WEAKNESS.

WE WILL STAND.

GOOD . . . . .

SO TELL ME, GENERALS . . . HAS THE CITY BEEN . . . ISOLATED?

WE CONTROL ALL THE SUPPLY ROUTES.

BUT SOMETHING IS TROUBLING US . . .

AS WE MARCHED OUR ARMY HERE TO TANEN GARD, WE NOTICED A NEW PLAGUE COVERS THE LAND -- EVIL RINGS OF DEATH THAT OUR HOLY MEN CALL GHOST CIRCLES.

DO NOT CONCERN YOURSELF.

NOW . . . TANEN GARD BELONGS TO THE DRAGONS --

-- VERY OLD AND IMPORTANT ALLIES OF THE ATHEIANS.

BY JOINING OUR ARMIES BETWEEN THEM, WE HAVE CUT OFF ANY ASSISTANCE THE CITY MAY HAVE HOPED FOR FROM THAT QUARTER.

WITHOUT THE DRAGONS THE ATHEIANS ARE NOTHING. WE WILL CRUSH THEM.

MY LORD, ABOUT THE PLAGUE --

I AM CONDUCTING THIS WAR, GENERAL. . . .

YOU SHOULD PREPARE YOUR SOLDIERS. WE WILL LEAVE A BATTALION **HERE** AT TANEN GARD. . . . OUR MAIN FORCE LEAVES **IMMEDIATELY** FOR ATHEIA.

YOU ARE **DISMISSED**.

NOT SO FAST.

WE SENT MANY OF OUR BRAVEST WARRIORS TO AID YOU IN YOUR ASSAULT ON **OLD MAN'S CAVE**.

AND YET, WE DO NOT SEE THEM HERE WITH YOU.

DID YOU **ABANDON** THEM IN THE GHOST CIRCLES?

REMEMBER OUR AGREEMENT, GENTLEMEN...

THE PAWA ARMY IS **MINE** TO COMMAND UNTIL WE SACK THE CITY.

IN RETURN... YOUR WARRIORS CAN PLUNDER ATHEIA FOR ALL HER **TREASURE.**

WE DIDN'T KNOW YOU WOULD **DESTROY** THE VALLEY.

oh, YOU DIDN'T? AND NOW YOU THINK THE TREASURE WON'T BE ENOUGH TO COMPENSATE YOU?

HMM? HE'S PROBABLY CHECKING ON BARTLEBY.

GET UP! WE HAVE TO FIND HIM!

OKAY, **OKAY!**

I DON'T LIKE THE IDEA OF ANY OF US BEING ALONE IN THE CITY. HERE, DON'T FORGET YOUR DISGUISE.

MY DISGUISE. . . I DON'T SEE HOW THIS IS SUPPOSED TO MAKE US **BLEND IN.** THIS HAT MAKES ME LOOK **RIDICULOUS!**

BOY, I'LL SAY! YOU LOOK LIKE AN **ACORN.**

IS THAT SO? AND WHAT ARE **YOU** SUPPOSED TO BE? A **LAWN GNOME?**

VERY FUNNY.

C'MON!

CREAK!

BARTLEBY?

HEY, I BROUGHT YOU SOME **BREAKFAST!**

SMILEY!

I WAS TAKIN' A NAP BY THE ROAD WHEN TWO LITTLE FELLOWS WITH **HUGE NOSES** STOLE OFF WITH IT!

A HAY CART **WAS** ALLOWED TO PASS THE GATES LAST EVENING, SIR, BUT AN OLD WOMAN AND HER GRANDDAUGHTER WERE DRIVING.

GO AWAY, FARMER. WE HAVE MORE SERIOUS MATTERS AT HAND THAN WORRYING ABOUT YOUR **HAY.**

BUT IT'S MY **WAGON!** HOW DO YOU EXPECT ME TO MAKE MY **LIVING?**

GET ALONG NOW, OR I'LL PUT YOUR LEGS IN IRON FOR YOU.

WHOA. SORRY!

BUZZ?

MY FAULT, MISS!

I HOPE I DIDN'T MESS UP YOUR NICE SOFT FUR.

UH... EXCUSE ME... I HAVE TO... UM...

PHONEY! WAIT UP!

THIS ISN'T WORTH THE RISK. THEY DON'T **USE** MONEY HERE!

OH, YEAH?

WELL, THE **TINGLING SENSATION** IN MY SCALP SAYS THEY **DO**!

LOOK! THERE'S A TRANSACTION TAKING PLACE **RIGHT NOW**.

ALL I SEE IS A BLANKET.

SHE'S **BUYING** THE BLANKET. SHE HASN'T PAID FOR IT YET. LET'S JUST **WATCH**!

ZZZZZ

SHE'LL PAY FOR IT WITH AN **EGG**, JUST LIKE EVERYWHERE **ELSE** IN THE VALLEY.

O, YE OF LITTLE FAITH...

POOKIE!

YES, MY LITTLE HONEY-COMB?

YOU PROMISED NO MORE STINGING PEOPLE.

YES, MY FLOWER.

POOKIE?

YOU **DID** IT! YOU CHASED THE BIG BULLY OFF! **BLESS YOU,** SIR!

THAT **ROUGHNECK BEE** IS THE TERROR OF THE **MARKET!**

EVER SINCE THE GHOST CIRCLES TRAPPED HIM INSIDE THE CITY, BUSINESS IS DOWN. FOLKS ARE TOO SCARED TO **SHOP!**

PLEASE ACCEPT THIS AS A TOKEN OF MY **GRATITUDE.**

YES, IT'S FROM ME AS WELL. PLEASE TAKE IT.

ME, TOO!

I DON'T BELIEVE IT! IS IT **GOLD?**

BUT THAT WOMAN PAID FOR HER BLANKET WITH AN **EGG.**

THIS EGG IS MY **BREAKFAST!** THEY ONLY PAY WITH EGGS OUT IN THE STICKS!

LISTEN, WE HAVE A PROPOSITION FOR YOU FELLOWS . . .

LOOK OVER THERE...

THE BEES WEREN'T SO BAD AT **FIRST**, WHEN THEY JUST SWARMED AROUND THE WELL ONCE A DAY TO **DRINK** . . .

BUT EVER SINCE THE GHOST CIRCLES POISONED THE WATER, THEY'VE BEEN NOTHING BUT **TROUBLE!**

WHAT DO YOU DRINK?

THE SOLDIERS HAVE A RESERVE WATER SUPPLY.

BUT THEY'RE **STINGY!** THEY ONLY HAND IT OUT IN THESE LITTLE, TINY JARS!

WHICH WE SELL **NEARLY EMPTY** TO THE BEES AT HIGH PRICES!

YES, **YES!** THAT BEE COMES HERE EVERY DAY AND LOSES HIS TEMPER. WE'LL GIVE YOU **MORE** GOLD COINS IF YOU COME BACK TOMORROW!

YES, TWENTY PIECES.

REALLY? I'LL **DO** IT!

WHAT? NO YOU WON'T!

THE QUEEN OF DREAMS SMILES UPON US ALL!

BLESS **YOU**, SIR!

NO PROBLEM! SEE YOU TOMORROW!

WHAT THEY'RE DOING TO THOSE BEES IS **TERRIBLE!**

A SIMPLE **DISTRIBUTION PROBLEM!** I'LL GIVE THE BEE A PIECE OF MY **FEE,** SO HE CAN PAY THE MERCHANTS! EVERYBODY'S **HAPPY,** AND I STILL MAKE A **KILLIN'!**

ON TOP OF **THAT,** MY SCALP IS **BIG** TINGLIN', FONE BONE!

THAT ONLY HAPPENS WHEN I'M ABOUT TO **SCORE BIG!**

FORGET THE GOLD. I'M NOT GONNA LET YOU JEOPARDIZE **THORN'S SAFETY.**

THIS HAS NOTHIN' TO DO WITH HER. I'LL HANDLE THE DEAL SO **EVERYBODY'S** HAPPY. I **PROMISE** NOTHIN'LL GO WRONG.

OF COURSE IT'S GONNA GO WRONG!

WHOA. WHOA, WAIT. IS THIS THE WAY WE CAME IN?

UH . . .

C'MON, WE'LL GO UP AND GET OUR BEARINGS.

ANYWAY, NOBODY'S GOING TO FIND OUT THAT THORN IS A PRINCESS IN DISGUISE --

PHONEY!

THIS IS SERIOUS. **YOU** HEARD THE OLD TEACHER LAST NIGHT! THERE'S BEEN SOME KIND OF A **TAKEOVER**. IF ANYONE FINDS OUT WHO SHE IS, IT'LL BE **DANGEROUS!**

YEAH, YEAH, AN' THE RAT CREATURES ARE COMIN', BUT WE'RE GONNA BE **LONG** GONE BEFORE ANY OF **THAT** HAPPENS.

IS THAT RIGHT?

YEP. WE'RE HANGIN' AROUND JUST LONG ENOUGH TO GET **MORE GOLD.**

JEEZ. HOW MUCH GOLD DO YOU NEED?

A LOT.

HEY - - LOOK AT **THIS** . . .

PLEASE.

COME IN.

HOW IS SHE? HAVE YOU KEPT HER AWAKE?

YES.

I MANAGED TO ROUND UP SOME WATER RATIONS, AND BROUGHT MERMIE WITH ME. SHE'S AN EXPERT IN HERBAL TEAS.

YOUR MAJESTY.

IT IS **ESSENTIAL** THAT WE KEEP THE PRINCESS AWAKE.

IT WILL BE MORE DIFFICULT FOR THE LOCUST IF HE CANNOT USE THE MEDIUM OF **DREAMS** TO CONTACT HER.

GOOD MORNING, YOUR HIGHNESS. WOULD YOU LIKE SOME TEA?

NO, THANK YOU, TEACHER.

ARE YOU SURE? YOU LOOK A BIT TIRED.

I'M SURE. THANK YOU.

HAVE SOME MORE TEA, THORN.

GRAN'MA, I'VE BEEN DRINKING TEA ALL NIGHT. IF I HAVE ANOTHER **DROP** I'M GOING TO THROW UP.

THE CHILD'S HEAD **IS** WARM.

MAYBE SHE NEEDS A BLANKET.

WOULD HER HIGHNESS LIKE THE WINDOW OPEN?

ARE YOU SURE YOU WOULDN'T LIKE SOME TEA?

WHAT I'D **LIKE** IS TO DISCUSS THE SITUATION IN THE CITY.

TSK. SHE'S SO YOUNG. IT'S NOT FAIR.

WHAT SHE REALLY NEEDS IS THE **SMELLY** TEA. GIVE ME THE BAG OF HERBS.

GOOD IDEA. THAT WILL KEEP HER AWAKE UNTIL THE MEETING TONIGHT!

RIGHT! WHERE WISER FOLK THAN US CAN DECIDE WHAT TO DO NEXT.

WOULD YOU LIKE HONEY IN YOUR TEA?

THUNK!

ENOUGH TEA.

NOW. . .

TELL ME ABOUT THIS EDICT OUTLAWING DRAGON LORE.

WHO IS RESPONSIBLE?

TARSIL, THE CAPTAIN OF THE QUEEN'S GUARD.

HE'S ALWAYS CHALLENGED THE DRAGONS' AUTHORITY.

HE EVEN LED AN EXPEDITION AS A YOUNG COMMANDER TO THE VERY EDGE OF THE DRAGONS' SACRED BURIAL GROUNDS.

BUT THE DRAGONS **PUNISHED** HIM. THEY **CRIPPLED** TARSIL FOR HIS IMPUDENCE.'

THERE WAS A SHORT BATTLE. THE DRAGONS GAVE FAIR WARNING BEFORE ATTACKING WITH OPEN FLAME.

TARSIL REPENTED, BUT HIS RESENTMENT IS WELL KNOWN.

WHEN THE GHOST CIRCLES FIRST APPEARED, HE OPENLY BLAMED THE DRAGONS AND ORDERED HIS SOLDIERS TO DESTROY ALL DRAGON SHRINES.

HE'S A **THUG.** CAN'T WE GET RID OF HIM?

HE'S SURROUNDED BY FIERCE AND LOYAL WARRIORS. . . WE COUNCIL MEMBERS ARE **OLD** AND FEEBLE. . .

WE HAVE ANOTHER PROBLEM. . .

TARSIL KNOWS ABOUT US.

FOR AWHILE HE WAS ONE OF THE PEOPLE I KEPT IN CONTACT WITH DURING OUR EXILE IN BARRELHAVEN.

HIS MEN WILL BE ON THE LOOKOUT FOR US.

YOU THINK HE'LL VIEW US AS A THREAT?

WE **ARE** A THREAT.

KRAK

GOOD.

AND WE HAVE THE ADVANTAGE AS LONG AS HE DOESN'T KNOW WE'RE HERE.

WOULD YOU LIKE SOME TEA, **NOW**?

YOU AND YOUR--! GET IT OUT OF HERE, OR I'LL MAKE YOU DRINK THE WHOLE **POT.**

WELL!

COME, MERMIE.

HMMPF.

SHE CERTAINLY TAKES AFTER **YOU. . .**

SEE YOU AT THE MEETING, OLD FRIEND.

EXACTLY.

BECAUSE OF US, TARSIL KNOWS GRAN'MA BEN AND THORN ARE IN THE CITY. WE HAVE TO **WARN** THEM!

WHAT ABOUT THE GIANT **BEE**? WE'RE GONNA NEED SMILEY'S HELP TO PROTECT THE PEDDLERS.

FORGET THE BEE! I TOLD YOU THAT PLAN IS GONNA **BACKFIRE!**

OKAY, FORGET THE BEE - -

LET'S FIGURE OUT WHERE THE PEDDLERS GOT ALL THIS **GOLD** TO PAY US FROM!

WHO CARES?

IT'S **GOLD,** FONE BONE! **GOLD!** WHERE DID THEY GET SO **MUCH** OF IT?!

WE'RE CAUGHT, PHONEY! SOLDIERS **INSIDE** THE WALLS AND RAT CREATURES **OUTSIDE!**

TRAPPED!

OKAY, OKAY. DON'T POP A BLOOD VESSEL.

I'LL GO GET SMILEY, YOU GO WARN THORN.

RIGHT. WE'LL RENDEZVOUS AT GRAN'MA BEN'S ROOM BEFORE THE UNDERGROUND MEETING.

AND **BE CAREFUL!** THERE'S STILL A LOT OF GUARDS LURKING ABOUT.

YES, MOTHER.

SMART ALEC.

IF HE GETS HIMSELF SURROUNDED BY SOLDIERS, HE'LL WISH HE LISTENED TO ME.

WHOOPS.

THORN? ARE YOU AWAKE IN THERE?

YES, GRAN'MA.

COME OUT ON THE BALCONY, THORN. THERE'S SOMEONE TO SEE YOU.

OUT HERE?

WHO . . . . ?

THORNY!

TED!

LOOK AT YOU-- SO **BEAUTIFUL!** I SWEAR YOU LOOKS MORE LIKE **MOON** EVER'DAY!

WELL, THANK YOU! THE MOON IS LOVELY!

No! No! NOT **THE** MOON! YOUR **MOTHER!** MOONWORT!

MOONWORT WAS HER NAME?

THAT WAS HER NICKNAME, DEAR. HER REAL NAME WAS LUNARIA.

QUEEN LUNARIA! DON'T YOU KNOW NOTHIN' ABOUT YER **MOTHER,** THORN?

NO, TED. TELL ME ABOUT HER.

YOUR MOTHER WAS KIND AN' BEAUTIFUL. SHE LOVED EVER'**ONE** AN' EVER'**THING**.

MORE!

SHE BELIEVED IN BUILDIN' THINGS LIKE LIBRARIES AN' PARKS. WHY, ALMOS' ALL THE **ART** AN' **PUBLIC GARDENS** IN ATHEIA WAS PUT UP BY HER.

THAT'S WONDERFUL!

WHAT ABOUT YOU, GRAN'MA? WHEN YOU WERE QUEEN, DID YOU BUILD ANYTHING?

WALLS.

I BUILT THE WALLS THAT SURROUND THE CITY.

TED, HOW LONG WILL IT TAKE FOR LUCIUS AND THE OTHERS TO REACH ATHEIA?

LUCIUS IS **ALIVE?**

OH, **YEAH!** THANKS TO **YOU** GOIN' AROUN' GATHERIN' UP FAMILIES, ALMOS' **EVER'ONE** IS STILL ALIVE!

THEY WAS ALL SAFE IN **OL' MAN'S CAVE** WHEN THE GHOST CIRCLES HIT!

LET'S NOT CELEBRATE JUST YET.... HOW LONG, TED?

I FIGGER LUCIUS AN' HIS WARRIORS WILL MOS' LIKELY REACH HERE IN **TWO DAYS.**

AND BRIAR?

I SEEN YER SISTER OUT WITH TH' RAT CREATURES OVER TO **TANEN GARD.** SHE JOININ' FORCES WITH TH' **PAWANS.**

WHOLE NASTY **ARMY** BE HERE EARLY AS **TOMORROW.**

BRIAR MADE IT THROUGH THE GHOST CIRCLES QUICKER THAN I THOUGHT.

TED, I NEED YOU TO TAKE A MESSAGE TO LUCIUS RIGHT AWAY.

YES, MA'AM.

TELL HIM WE'LL HOLD OFF BRIAR'S ARMY AS LONG AS WE CAN – –

ON THE SECOND NIGHT FROM TONIGHT, HAVE LUCIUS POSITION HIS MEN BEHIND THE RAT CREATURES – – OPPOSITE THE **WEST GATE. . .**

. . . WHEN HE'S READY, HAVE HIM LIGHT A TORCH UP ON **SINNER'S ROCK.** WHEN WE SEE THAT SIGNAL, WE'LL CHARGE OUT THE GATE – – TRAPPING THE ENEMY BETWEEN US!'

YOU **GOTS** AN ARMY, GRAM?

NOT YET. BUT WE'RE HAVING A MEETING OF THE UNDERGROUND TONIGHT.

OKEE-DOKEY, THEN. SECOND NIGHT, SIGNAL FIRE UP ON SINNER'S ROCK. **GOT IT.**

BY THE WEST GATE, TED, THAT'S IMPORTANT. WE'LL KEEP BRIAR'S MAIN FORCE THERE IF WE CAN.

I'M ON MY WAY.

SEE YA, THORNY! GOOD LUCK!

YOU TOO, TED. GOOD-BYE!

GRAN'MA, WE DON'T HAVE AN ARMY.

NOT YET.

ARE YOU SURE THIS IS A GOOD PLAN, THEN?

NO...

IT ONLY DEALS WITH THE PROBLEMS WE HAVE **OUTSIDE** THE WALLS...

...INSIDE, WE STILL HAVE **TARSIL THE USURPER** TO DEAL WITH.

CRACK!

SIT DOWN, SIT DOWN! WE'RE HAVING BLANK SANDWICHES.

BLANK SANDWICHES?

FIRST, WE CUT A SLICE OF BREAD -- AND **REMOVE** THE CRUST...

WATCH IT! IT'S KINDA TRICKY.

THERE. NOW HOLD YOUR BREAD LIKE THIS . . .

NOW PUT 'EM TOGETHER AND YOU HAVE A **BLANK SANDWICH!**

MAKE **ME** ONE, SMILEY!

FORTUNATELY, NOT EVEN **YOU** CAN DAMPEN MY SPIRITS TODAY...

WHYN'T?

BECAUSE TODAY I'VE GOT **GOLD!**

WHOA.

ME AN' FONE BONE CHASED A BEE OUT OF THE MARKET SQUARE, AND THE MERCHANTS REWARDED US WITH **TWENTY PIECES OF GOLD!**

JUST FOR CHASIN' OFF A **BEE?**

IT WAS A **BIG** BEE, BUT GUESS WHAT? THEY'LL PAY US TWENTY GOLD COINS **EVERY MORNING** IF WE'LL COME BACK AND KEEP THE BEE AWAY!

NO KIDDIN'?

NO KIDDIN'. **SO...** DO YOU THINK YOU CAN REWORK THESE COINS AND PUT MY FACE ON 'EM?

SURE. GOLD'S A SOFT METAL AN' WE'VE GOT HAMMERS. I CAN RIG UP A STRIKE OPERATION, NO SWEAT.

GOOD! 'CAUSE A LEADER **HAS** TO HAVE COINS WITH HIS **FACE** ON 'EM!

NATCH! BUT ARE THEY REALLY GONNA MAKE YOU THEIR LEADER JUST FOR CHASIN' OFF A **BEE?**

THESE POOR PEOPLE ARE LONGING FOR A PROTECTOR. SOMEONE TO LOOK OUT FOR THEIR BEST INTERESTS...

SOMEONE TO BE THEIR **KING.**

WAAAAIT A MINUTE... DID YOU FIND THE TREASURE?

NOT YET. BUT IT MUST BE **HUGE!** LOOK WHAT THEY CAN AFFORD TO PAY JUST TO SWAT A BEE!

DO YOU THINK WHOEVER IS **KING** GETS TO KEEP THE TREASURE?

OF **COURSE!** THAT'S THE WHOLE POINT OF BEING KING!

WHOA, WHOA. IF GRAN'MA BEN IS **QUEEN**, DOESN'T THE TREASURE BELONG TO **HER?**

NAH, SHE'S **RETIRED.** AND THORN'S JUST A PRINCESS.

BESIDES, I'M ONLY GONNA BE KING FOR A COUPLE OF DAYS.

JUST LONG ENOUGH TO CLAIM THE TREASURE, HUH?

RIGHT! THEN WE'RE SPLITTIN' FOR **BONEVILLE,** BECAUSE WE DON'T WANT TO BE HERE WHEN THE RAT CREATURES SHOW UP.

SPEAKING OF WHICH, I BETTER GET OVER TO GRAN'MA'S ROOM FOR THE UNDERGROUND MEETING.

SEE YA, PHONEY!

OH, BOY! THIS IS **IT!** WE'RE FINALLY GOIN' HOME TO **BONE - -**

- - VILLE.

THE PAWANS AND THE RAT CREATURES ARE WORKING **TOGETHER**...

... THIS IS NOT A TRADE EMBARGO, GUILD MASTER. THIS IS AN ACT OF **WAR**.

LORD TARSIL, IF I MAY SPEAK ON BEHALF OF THE MERCHANT HOUSES...

...THERE ARE MANY IN THE GUILD WHO BELIEVE THE PAWAN ARMY WOULD END ITS BLOCKADE OF OUR TRADE ROUTES IF YOU **RELAXED** YOUR BAN ON DRAGON LORE --

WHAT YOU ARE SAYING IS **HERESY**, GUILD MASTER.

NOW, NOW...

ONLY IN THE PROVINCES! MANY OF THE MERCHANTS FEEL WE COULD **WIN** THE COMMON PEOPLE AND ROB THE PAWAN ARMY OF LOCAL SUPPORT. THE BLOCKADE WOULD **CRUMBLE**.

NORMALLY, WE WOULDN'T **DREAM** OF ASKING SUCH A THING, YOUR WORSHIP-- EVERYONE ON THE COUNCIL **KNOWS** OF YOUR GREAT SACRIFICE --

B-- BUT EVERY DAY THE BLOCKADE CONTINUES THE MERCHANTS ARE LOSING **MONEY.**

WHAT THE DRAGONS HAVE DONE TO ME, THEY **MEAN** TO DO TO OUR WHOLE WAY OF LIFE.

THEY ARE **CORRUPT** BEINGS. THEY LIVE IN THE EARTH LIKE **WORMS** . . .

THEY ARE NOT OF THE LIGHT . . .

LIKE YOU . . .

. . . OR ME.

THEY EAT OUR LIGHT.

LORD TARSIL!

YES?

YOUR GREATNESS, JUST AS YOU PREDICTED, TWO OF THE **BONE** CREATURES HAVE BEEN SPOTTED IN THE CITY.

SOLDIERS ARE SEARCHING NEAR THE OLD SQUARE NOW.

THE QUEEN.

WHAT OF THE QUEEN AND HER GRANDDAUGHTER . . ? THE HEIR TO THE THRONE?

AN OLD WOMAN AND HER GRANDDAUGHTER ENTERED THE WEST GATE LAST NIGHT, BUT THEIR WHEREABOUTS ARE UNKNOWN.

PUT MORE SOLDIERS ON THE STREET. . .

FIND THOSE BONE CREATURES. . .

ONCE THEY LEAD YOU TO THE PRINCESS, **ARREST** HER AND BRING HER TO ME.

THE CHARGES, MY LORD?

HERESY, SERGEANT AT ARMS. . .

IT IS AGAINST THE LAW TO WORSHIP **DRAGONS** AND SHE SHALL BE BURNED AT THE STAKE UNTIL DEAD.

THORN! GET AWAY FROM THAT WINDOW.

GRAN'MA, WHAT'S GOING ON? SOLDIERS ARE SWARMING ALL OVER THE STREETS.

I'M NOT SURE, BUT IT CAN'T BE GOOD. TAKE YOUR SHAWL. WE HAVE TO GET TO THE MEETING.

WE CAN'T LEAVE YET... FONE BONE'S NOT HERE.

WHAT DO YOU **MEAN** HE'S NOT HERE? HE SHOULD HAVE BEEN HERE A LONG **TIME AGO**!

BAM!

COULD HE HAVE GOTTEN LOST, PHONEY?

WE GOT LOST THIS MORNING, BUT I THOUGHT HE KNEW HIS WAY FROM THE MARKET SQUARE.

WE HAVE TO GO FIND HIM.

NOT NOW. THE LIVES OF EVERYONE IN THE CITY DEPEND ON OUR MEETING TONIGHT. I'LL SEND MERMIE OUT TO LOOK FOR FONE BONE.

MERMIE? THE **TEA** LADY?

MERMIE IS A SEVENTH LEVEL DREAM-MASTER. SHE CAN HANDLE IT.

NOW LET'S GO-- AND KEEP YOUR HEADS DOWN . . .

YOUR HIGHNESS, EVERYONE IS WAITING.

MERMIE, FONE BONE IS MISSING -- LOST OR WORSE. SEE IF YOU CAN FIND HIM, PLEASE.

RIGHT AWAY.

TEACHER . . .

I DON'T WANT A REPEAT OF LAST NIGHT. DID YOU FIGURE OUT WHAT THAT **COLD** SPOT WAS ?

YES, A GHOST CIRCLE WAS FORMING HERE IN THE MIDDLE OF MY KITCHEN. YOUR SISTER BRIAR WAS ATTEMPTING TO REACH THROUGH OUR DEFENSES.

SHE CAN **DO** THAT? BRIAR CAN CONTROL GHOST CIRCLES, NOW?

WE CAN, TOO, TO AN EXTENT. WHEN THE GHOST CIRCLES FIRST APPEARED FROM THE NORTH, WE USED **PRAYER STONES** TO TURN THEM BACK.

YOU MUST HAVE USED A LOT OF PRAYER STONES.

I THINK WE **SAW** THAT LINE OF GHOST CIRCLES YOU TURNED BACK. IS THAT POSSIBLE?

IT'S POSSIBLE. . . WE SENT THE WHOLE FRONT LINE BOUNCING BACK TOWARD YOU.

FOR TONIGHT'S MEETING, WE'VE SURROUNDED THE ENTIRE KITCHEN WITH PRAYER STONES.

I'M VERY IMPRESSED, OLD FRIEND. I FEEL SAFER ALREADY.

DON'T THANK ME YET. WAIT UNTIL YOU FIND OUT WHOSE LORE WAS ACTUALLY RESPONSIBLE.

QUEEN ROSE. . .

I'LL COME RIGHT TO THE POINT. MY SISTER BRIAR IS STILL ALIVE AND IS LEADING AN INVASION FORCE THAT COULD BE HERE AS EARLY AS TOMORROW MORNING.

I KNOW TARSIL HAS TAKEN CONTROL OF OUR **ARMY**, BUT HOW SMART IS HE? CAN HE DEFEND THE CITY AGAINST AN **ATTACK?**

WE HAVE SEEN HIS SOLDIERS BRINGING ANIMALS AND FODDER INSIDE THE MAIN WALLS, AND HE HAS BEGUN RATIONING **WATER.**

INTERESTING. . . WHEN I FIRST ARRIVED, I NOTICED THAT MOST OF THE FORTIFICATIONS HAD BEEN **REBUILT- -**

GOOD. HE'S PREPARING FOR A SIEGE.

IN DIRECT **VIOLATION** OF THE TREATY WE SIGNED WITH THE RAT CREATURES, I SHOULD POINT OUT!

WELL, AT LEAST **SOME** OF THE TRAINING I GAVE HIM WASN'T WASTED.

WHAT ABOUT THE SOLDIERS THEMSELVES?

POORLY TRAINED AND **BADLY** DISCIPLINED. A SMALL GROUP OF FANATICS KNOWN AS **THE VEDU** ENFORCE TARSIL'S RULE.

THE REST ARE EITHER MERCENARIES OR LOYAL TO THE OLD KINGDOM.

I BELIEVE THEY ARE **ALL** LOYAL. IF WE TOLD THEM THAT YOU HAD **RETURNED,** THEY WOULD TURN ON THE USURPER AND **KILL** HIM.

HAS ANYONE BOTHERED TO **TALK** WITH THIS TARSIL? WE HAVE A COMMON ENEMY, PERHAPS WE COULD **COOPERATE** - -

Tch.

JUST LIKE YOUR MOTHER.

WHAT ABOUT THE **TREASURY**? IF WE HAD **THAT**, TARSIL WOULD LOSE HIS HOLD ON THE MERCENARIES. HE COULDN'T **PAY** THEM.

TRUE . . .

. . . BUT TARSIL KNOWS THIS. HE'S **HIDDEN** THE TREASURE WHERE NO ONE CAN FIND IT.

THEN WE'D BETTER PLAY THE **LOYALTY CARD**. HEADMASTER, SPREAD THE WORD THROUGH THE RANKS **THIS VERY NIGHT THE QUEEN HAS RETURNED** - -

WAIT! DID YOU HEAR THAT?

SOMEONE IS COMING!

IT'S FONE BONE!

OKAY.

THEY WENT PAST US.

BUT I THINK WE'RE STUCK HERE FOR A WHILE -- I HOPE PHONEY GOT AWAY.

I HOPE THE OTHER MEMBERS OF THE RESISTANCE GOT AWAY.

FONE BONE, YOU SHOULDN'T HAVE BEEN SO **ROUGH** PULLING THE HEADMASTER THROUGH THE WINDOW!

SORRY. I THOUGHT GETTING **CAUGHT** AND THROWN IN A DUNGEON WOULD'VE BEEN WORSE.

THIS MAN IS THE GREATEST LIVING DREAM-MASTER. **SHOW SOME RESPECT!**

HE SAID HE WAS SORRY, GRAN'MA.

I'M FINE.

SO THIS IS FONE BONE . . . THE LITTLE **CREATURE** WHO HAS COME INTO OUR VALLEY AND **AWAKENED** THE SLEEPING PRINCESS.

WELL . . .

IT REMAINS TO BE SEEN, MR. BONE FROM BONEVILLE . . .

WHETHER YOU HAVE **SAVED** US . . .

. . . OR DESTROYED US.

WHAT'S **THAT** SUPPOSED TO MEAN?

MASTER. . . IT'S UNFAIR TO BLAME FONE BONE. THORN WAS **BOUND** TO LEARN THE TRUTH. IT WAS UNAVOIDABLE.

BY THE TIME FONE BONE WANDERED ONTO OUR FARM, THE GREAT RED DRAGON HAD BEEN TRYING FOR **YEARS** TO CONVINCE ME TO TELL HER.

THE RAT CREATURES WERE DEFYING THE **TREATY**, BUT I WAS TOO STUBBORN TO LISTEN.

THE DRAGON WAS RIGHT. AS MUCH AS I WISHED TO PROTECT HER, IT IS THORN'S DESTINY TO REBUILD THE KINGDOM.

I AGREE THE FAILURE IS YOURS, BUT THE BURDEN IS HERS.

AND SHE HAS HAD NO **TRAINING**.

SHE WILL BE TESTED.

SORELY TESTED, I'M AFRAID, AS ARE ALL WHO ARE CHOSEN.

BUT SHE HAS REACHED THE TURNING WITHOUT ANY TRAINING, AND I AM CONCERNED THAT SHE WILL **FAIL.**

MASTER, IF YOU HAD SEEN WHAT THIS YOUNG WOMAN HAS BEEN THROUGH, AND HOW SHE HAS **HANDLED** HERSELF, YOU WOULD BE LESS WORRIED.

I HAVE **HEARD** ABOUT THESE ESCAPADES. WRESTLING WITH THE LOCUST **HIMSELF --** TEARING OFF A PIECE OF HIS **BLACK SOUL** AND KEEPING IT WITHIN HER BOSOM!

DON'T YOU SEE HOW **DANGEROUS** THIS IS, YOUR MAJESTY?

THE TWO WORLDS OF THE DREAMING ARE **OUT OF BALANCE . . .**

THE VEIL THAT SEPARATES THIS WORLD FROM THE NEXT HAS BEEN **PIERCED,** AND GHOST CIRCLES HAVE BEGUN TO POOL AND FORM . . .

--THE DRAGONS HAVE GONE UNDERGROUND AND LEFT US --

THESE ARE THE **END TIMES,** AND SHE IS THE **VENI-YAN-CARI.**

IF **SHE** FAILS - -

IT WILL BE **CATASTROPHIC.**

WAIT - - WHAT IF I DIDN'T **TAKE** THIS TEST? WOULD THAT STOP THE DISASTER FROM HAPPENING? COULD WE STOP THE WAR?

IN LIFE, TESTS COME UPON ONE UNANNOUNCED AND WITHOUT WARNING.

BUT YOU KNOW THAT . . . YOU ARE THE AWAKENED ONE.

THAT'S WHAT **VENI-YAN-CARI** MEANS, THE AWAKENED ONE.

WISDOM.

BAH! TAKE HER BACK TO THE FARM. HER PRESENCE HERE MAKES THE SITUATION FAR TOO DANGEROUS - -

BRING HER BACK **AFTER** WE REBUILD THE KINGDOM.

WHO TH' HECK **IS** THIS GUY?

AND **YOU!** WHAT ARE **YOU** DOIN' COW-TOWIN' TO THIS **NUTTY OLD FOP?** YOU'RE THE **QUEEN!**

BONE!

WHO DOES HE THINK HE **IS?** WE DIDN'T NEED HIS HELP **BEFORE**, AN' WE DON'T NEED IT **NOW.**

I HAVE A GREAT DEAL MORE EXPERIENCE IN THESE MATTERS THAN **YOU**, YOUNG MAN.

THAT'S HARD TO BELIEVE -- HAVE YOU EVER BEEN **INSIDE** A GHOST CIRCLE AND TALKED TO DEAD PEOPLE? **WE HAVE.**

DEAD PEOPLE?

FONE BONE . . . ?

I THOUGHT WE WEREN'T GOING TO SHARE THAT.

SORRY, THAT WAS RASH. BUT THIS GUY DOESN'T KNOW **JACK.**

WHAT ARE YOU TWO TALKING ABOUT? WHEN DID THIS HAPPEN?

IMPOSSIBLE! NO ONE BUT THE DRAGONS CAN TALK TO THE **DEAD!**

DOES THIS MEAN YOU **BELIEVE** ME, EVEN THOUGH YOU COULDN'T HEAR THEIR VOICES YOURSELF?

OF **COURSE** I BELIEVE YOU.

WELL, I **DO NOT!** VOICES IN A GHOST CIRCLE?

BAH!

ONLY DRAGONS SPEAK TO THE DEAD. NO **HUMAN** CAN TRAVEL TO **THAT** DEPTH OF THE DREAMING AND RETURN.

EVER.

I DON'T KNOW WHAT **DEPTH** THE CIRCLE TOOK US TO, BUT MY DEAD MOTHER SENT THIS MESSAGE . . .

SEEK THE CROWN OF HORNS.

WHAT'S GOING ON?

WE BROKE UP A MEETING OF DRAGON WORSHIPPERS EARLIER--

SOME OF THEM MIGHT'VE RUN THIS WAY TRYING TO ESCAPE.

SEEN ANYONE?

JUST THIS CRAZY OLD FARMER WHO CLAIMS HIS **HAY CART** WAS STOLEN. HE WANTS IN TO FIND IT.

WELL, RUN HIM OFF.

LISTEN--

THERE'S WORD GOING AROUND THAT THE **QUEEN** HERSELF WAS AT THE MEETING.

THEY MAY BE PLANNING AN INSURRECTION.

SO STAY ALERT.

BLOODY STARS. HALF THE MEN ARE IN THE TOWERS **NOW** WATCHING FOR AN ATTACK FROM **PAWA**-- NOW **THIS**?

I HOPE YOU CATCH THOSE DRAGON-LOVERS AND RIP THEIR **GUTS** OUT.

DON'T WORRY. THEY WON'T GET AWAY.

PSSST!

SMILEY, ARE YOU IN HERE? WE GOTTA--

HOW'S THAT ONE?

PERFECT! ONE MORE TO GO!

WHAT ARE YOU DOING?!

WE'RE SMASHING!

WE MADE A STAMP WITH YOUR FACE ON IT, PHONEY...

LOOK!

BARTLEBY IS SO STRONG, HE CAN STRIKE IT IN THE GOLD WITH ONE HIT!

THIS IS THE HAPPIEST DAY OF MY LIFE.

YOU **LIKE?**

I **LOVE!**

LISTEN -- I KNOW WHERE THE **TREASURE** IS!

BUT WE HAVE TO **HURRY** BEFORE THE STREETS GET TOO CROWDED.

HOT DOG! LEMME GET MY **HAT!**

No, No, No---- YOU STAY HERE, BARTLEBY!

AND **KEEP QUIET!** SOLDIERS ARE LOOKING FOR US. IF THEY FIND A BABY RAT CREATURE, WE'RE **DEAD MEAT!**

GEE, PHONEY, IF IT'S **THAT** DANGEROUS, MAYBE WE SHOULD LAY LOW. . .

I'M **NOT** GOING BACK TO BONEVILLE EMPTY-HANDED!

IMPOSSIBLE!

NO ONE, NOT EVEN THE **ROYAL FAMILY** KNOWS ABOUT THE CROWN OF HORNS.

IT IS THE DRAGONS' **GREATEST SECRET.**

YOU SEEM TO KNOW ABOUT IT.

YOU MAKE **LIGHT**, YOUNG MAN, BUT EVEN AMONG THE **HOLY**, ALMOST NOTHING IS KNOWN ABOUT THIS SACRED OBJECT.

YOUR HIGHNESS, IF IT PLEASES YOU, I WOULD LIKE TO HEAR YOUR STORY ABOUT TALKING TO THE DEAD.

ACTUALLY, THE FARMERS I SPOKE WITH WERE NOT DEAD. THEY WERE **BETWEEN** LIFE AND DEATH . . .

WHICH IS WHAT MAKES THEIR SITUATION SO UNBEARABLE.

BUT I'M **CONVINCED** THE GHOST CIRCLES AREN'T FULLY FORMED AND WE STILL HAVE TIME TO RESCUE THESE POOR PEOPLE.

MY MOTHER MUST HAVE THOUGHT THE CROWN OF HORNS WOULD HELP US.

I HOPE **I** CAN HELP YOU PRINCESS. ALMOST NOTHING IS KNOWN ABOUT THIS OBJECT. NO ONE HAS EVER **SEEN** IT.

BUT... I WILL TELL YOU WHAT LITTLE I **DO** KNOW --

THE CROWN OF HORNS SITS DIRECTLY UPON THE VEIL, HALF IN OUR WORLD, AND HALF IN THE **DREAMING** WORLD.

IT IS THE TIPPING POINT -- THE POINT OF **BALANCE.**

SOME SAY IT IS THE VERY **HEART** OF OUR WORLD.

HMM. THE GHOST CIRCLES MIGHT VANISH IF WE COULD RESTORE **BALANCE.**

YEAH, BUT **HOW?**

ALL WE HAVE TO DO IS **FIND** THE CROWN OF HORNS AND TIP IT BACK INTO PLACE.

WISDOM.

NO, NO, NO, **NO.** DON'T YOU SEE?

THIS IS EXACTLY THE LACK OF TRAINING I WAS **TALKING** ABOUT! DO YOU KNOW WHAT WOULD **HAPPEN** IF SHE EVEN **TOUCHED** THIS SACRED OBJECT?

HOW WOULD **I** KNOW?

SHE'S A **VENI-YAN-CARI** WHO CARRIES A PIECE OF THE LOCUST'S SPIRIT WITHIN HER BREAST. **TWO OPPOSING FORCES OF ENERGY TOGETHER** - -

THE SLIGHTEST CONTACT WITH THE CROWN OF HORNS WOULD CAUSE A TREMENDOUS DISRUPTION.'

ALL OF EXISTENCE WOULD FLICKER LIKE A CANDLE - - PERHAPS EVEN **GO OUT!**

HMM. NOT QUITE SO MUCH WISDOM AS YOU THOUGHT.

NEW PLAN.

RIGHT. IF WE'RE GONNA DO THIS THE **OLD-FASHIONED** WAY, WE BETTER GET STARTED. THE SUN'S ALREADY UP.

MASTER, YOU SPREAD THE WORD AMONG THE LOYAL TO GATHER AT THE FRONT GATE. HAVE THEM BRING ANY WEAPON THEY CAN.

THORN, YOU AND I ARE GOING TO PAY AN EARLY MORNING VISIT TO OUR TYRANT FRIEND, **TARSIL.**

FONE BONE, YOU MAKE SURE YOUR COUSIN PHONEY BONE STAYS OUT OF **TROUBLE.**

WHY DO **I** ALWAYS GET THE HARDEST JOB?

OKAY, OKAY- - C'MERE!

AT THE MEETING LAST NIGHT THEY WERE TALKING ABOUT TARSIL **RATIONING** THE **WATER SUPPLY!**

LOOK!

SO?

IF THE CITY HAS A **WELL,** YOU DON'T **NEED** TO RATION THE WATER! NOT WHEN THERE ISN'T A **DROUGHT!**

AND **THEN** THEY TALKED ABOUT TARSIL HIDING THE CITY'S **TREASURE** WHERE **NO ONE CAN FIND IT!**

MAYBE IT'S THE GHOST CIRCLES. THEY COULD'VE RUINED THE WATER SO THEY'D HAVE TO SEAL TH' WELL SHUT.

WHEN WE WERE OUT IN THE GHOST CIRCLES, THORN TOLD US THAT ONLY **SURFACE** WATER WAS RUINED - - EVERYTHING **UNDERGROUND** WAS **SAFE!**

AH?!

COME ON!

UM . . . PHONEY? HOW COME THE MARKET SQUARE IS SO EMPTY?

WHAT ARE YOU TALKIN' ABOUT - -

WAIT A MINUTE. YOU'RE RIGHT. THIS TIME YESTERDAY, THE PLACE WAS PACKED.

STRANGE.

MAYBE IT'S A HOLIDAY!

NO, SOMETHING'S WRONG.

YOO-HOO! HELLO, MR. BONE!

OH, GREAT. IT'S THE GUY WHO HIRED ME TO CHASE OFF THE BEE. C'MON, LET'S DITCH HIM.

HAVEN'T YOU HEARD THE RUMORS ABOUT THE INVASION?

WHAT RUMORS?

WORD ON THE STREET SAYS THE PAWANS ARE COMING. THEY MIGHT ATTACK TODAY!

WHAT? ATTACK HERE?

YES! MAYBE EVEN THIS MORNING! I WAS SO WORRIED YOU WEREN'T GOING TO COME AND PROTECT MY WARES!

WELL, I SUPPOSE, IF YOU'VE GOT THE MONEY...

NOW, I'VE ALREADY SET UP MY **JARS** OVER THERE. THEY'RE VERY **VALUABLE!** - - BLACK MARKET WATER AT VERY AFFORDABLE PRICES, FROM THE SOLDIERS' OWN RESERVES - -

TROUBLE IS, OF COURSE, WATER IS WHAT ATTRACTS THE **BEES!**

YOU'RE WORRIED ABOUT **BEES** WHEN INVADERS ARE COMING? THERE'S NO **CUSTOMERS!**

IT'S STILL **DANGEROUS!** I'VE GOT ALL THIS **WATER**, AND THE BEES COULD SPOT ALL THIS **WATER** ANY TIME NOW!

EXCUSE ME, PHONEY, CAN I TALK TO YOU FOR A MINUTE?

WE HAVE TO LEAVE **NOW**. DO NOT PASS **GO**, DO NOT COLLECT ANY PROTECTION FEES FROM CRAZY PEOPLE.

SIGH.

I GUESS YOU'RE RIGHT- -

BUT WHAT ABOUT THE **BURIED** TREASURE?

THERE YOU ARE! WHERE ARE THE GUARDS?

COMING! THEY WERE BUSY BREAKING UP A GANG OF DRAGON WORSHIPPERS.

THE BONES ARE HERE **NOW**, BUT WITHOUT ANY **BEES** I'M AFRAID THEY'RE GONNA LEAVE!

STALL THEM! IF THEY GET AWAY, WE WON'T GET THE **REWARD MONEY!**

OR THE MONEY BACK THAT WE GAVE THEM YESTERDAY- - HEY! WHERE'D THEY GO?

JUST A QUICK **PEEK**, NOW, AND IF THE TREASURE'S **IN THERE**, WE'LL GET IT **LATER**, ALL RIGHT?

SURE, SURE! I PROMISE. JUST A PEEK!

WE DON'T HAVE MUCH — —

LOOK!

ISN'T THAT THE **MARKET SQUARE**?!

BZ! BZ!

IT'S **PHONEY**! HE'S IN TROUBLE!

ooh——

WE DON'T HAVE TIME FOR THIS.

GUARD! LET ME IN! I WANT MY **HAY CART**!

WE HAVE TO **SAVE HIM**!

I'LL SAVE HIM — — YOU BOTH STAY HERE AND **DON'T MOVE**!

I THOUGHT I TOLD YOU TO GO HOME!

BUT MY HAY CART WAS STOLEN!

YOU KNOW THE RULES. YOU CAN'T GET IN WITHOUT A PERMIT.

HEY, GUARD! THAT KID IS BUILDING A DRAGON SHRINE!

DON'T THE RULES APPLY TO HER?

GRAN'MA, THAT LITTLE GIRL WHO HELPED US — — **TANEAL** — — SHE'S SETTING UP A SHRINE RIGHT IN FRONT OF A SOLDIER!

THORN, GET DOWN BEHIND THE PARAPET AND STAY PUT UNTIL I GET BACK!

...TO BE CONTINUED.

About JEFF SMITH

JEFF SMITH was born and raised in the American Midwest and learned about cartooning from comic strips, comic books, and watching animated shorts on TV. After four years of drawing comic strips for The Ohio State University's student newspaper and co-founding Character Builders animation studio in 1986, Smith launched the comic book *BONE* in 1991. Between *BONE* and other comics projects, Smith spends much of his time on the international guest circuit promoting comics and the art of graphic novels.

More about *BONE*

An instant classic when it first appeared in the U.S. as an underground comic book in 1991, *BONE* has since garnered 38 international awards and sold millions of copies in 15 languages. Now, Scholastic's GRAPHIX imprint is publishing full-color graphic novel editions of the nine-book *BONE* series. Look for the continuing adventures of the Bone cousins in *Crown of Horns*.

Dreaming of Harvestar